THE
FORGOTTEN
ROOM

For Jesse, Dylan & Riley, Claire & Ted,
and Daniel; chaos begins at home.

THE FORGOTTEN ROOM

MYSTERIES OF ECKERT HOUSE

by CHRIS AUER

smarter • stronger
2:52
deeper • cooler

Zonderkidz

Zonder**kidz**®

The children's group of Zondervan

www.zonderkidz.com

The Forgotten Room
Copyright © 2005 by Chris Auer

Requests for information should be addressed to:
Grand Rapids, Michigan 49530

Library of Congress Cataloging-in-Publication Data

Auer, Chris, 1955-
   The forgotten room / by Chris Auer.
      p. cm.-(2:52 mysteries of Eckert House ; bk. 4)
   Summary: Eleven-year old Dan helps discover the whereabouts of a long-lost
golden room, worth hundreds of millions of dollars, and devises a plan to keep it
safe until a decision about its true ownership can be made.
   ISBN 0-310-70873-7 (softcover : alk. paper)
   [1. Lost and found possessions—Fiction. 2. Gold—Fiction. 3. Museums—
Fiction. 4. Christian life—Fiction. 5. Mystery and detective stories.] I. Title. II.
Series.
   PZ7.A9113Fo 2005
   [Fic]--dc22

                                                                2004024585

Zonderkidz is a trademark of Zondervan

Editor: Amy DeVries
Cover design: Jay Smith–Juicebox Designs
Interior design: Susan Ambs
Art direction: Michelle Lenger and Merit Alderink

Printed in the United States of America

05 06 07 /❖DCI/ 10 9 8 7 6 5 4 3 2 1

CONTENTS

REFLECTIONS

Dan Pruitt stood in the park looking out across the Morgan River. It was early October and the brilliant gold, orange, and red of the leaves over his head matched the glowing gold, orange, and red of the setting sun.

"Nice work," Dan said aloud. He was talking to God, and he was absolutely sincere. "Maybe even better than yesterday."

Dan had discovered that he was not one of those people who could kneel at his bedside every night, fold his hands, and pray to a distant God up in the clouds. No, at twelve years old, Dan preferred a conversation that lasted the entire day and included comments like the one he had just made. At night he did take time to reflect on his day and offer a more formal prayer, but the relaxed approach was his usual style.

Dan turned away from the river and headed back across the park toward Eckert House. He knew his family would be there shortly, for they were going out to dinner to celebrate his little brother, Jack's, birthday. Dan stopped for a moment to look at Eckert House as its front windows reflected the brilliant colors of the evening sky.

Eckert House was once the home of the wealthiest family in the town of Freemont, Pennsylvania, but when their large fortune was all spent, the family gave the mansion and all that was in it to the town. It was restored and turned into a museum, a museum that was now famous, in part, because of Dan.

Dan had accidentally uncovered a valuable statue of a bronze angel that he had nicknamed Loretta. As a result both Eckert House and Dan were known all over the country.

Being on television and in national magazines had been the high point of the past summer, but as Dan passed a large granite monument, the town's war memorial, he was also reminded of one of the summer's low points. Dan stopped. He had almost died on this spot.

"Thanks," Dan whispered in prayer, remembering how he had been saved from Rick Doheny, the desperate man who had tried to kill him and was now in jail. The past summer had been full of dangers that Dan was happy to forget. Now things like watching a sunset or going out for pizza with his family, things that he had never given much thought to before, were suddenly very important to him.

The war memorial was an important marker to Dan for another reason, too. On it, he was sure, was the solution to a mystery he had been trying to solve all summer.

All the soldiers from Freemont who had died during a war had their names chiseled into the large granite monument. One of those men was the father of a boy who had written a diary during World War Two that Dan had been investigating. He was trying to uncover the boy's identity.

In the diary, the boy had written his deepest and most personal feelings. He was very honest about his fear that his father would be killed in the war, a fear that Dan felt had come true, for the diary abruptly stopped in April of 1945, just before the war in Europe ended. The boy's father had been fighting there. Dan concluded that the father's death was why the boy never finished the diary.

The woman in charge of Eckert House, Miss Alma Louise Stockton LeMay, had given the diary to Dan and asked him to solve the mystery of its author. She also asked Dan to find out, if possible, how it came to be in a box in the attic of Eckert House, for it seemed to have no connection to anyone who had ever lived there.

Miss Alma was older than seventy, but less than a hundred. She weighed no more than ninety pounds, but could make grown men three times her size tremble with fear. She was a terror, a person whom you did not want as an enemy.

Just the week before, she had refused to meet with a real-life prince who had come thousands of miles to

Eckert House for a visit. He was twenty-three minutes late for his appointment. Miss Alma told him to come again another day—after he had bought himself a new watch. Dan liked her very much.

Across the street Dan saw his mother pull up, roll down the window of her car and wave to him.

"I'll be back in five minutes. I have to get your sisters," she called.

In the front seat was Dan's Grandpa Mike. This was the first time he'd been out of the house for something other than a doctor's appointment since he'd had a stroke earlier in the year. Grandpa Mike still walked very slowly with a special cane, but his speech was getting much better. There were times when he could speak whole sentences now. Dan waved back. Grandpa Mike also waved.

"Well," said Dan for what he felt was the millionth time as he gazed up at the monument, "the name of that boy's father is right here. The solution to the mystery is right in front of me."

Dan was not alone in trying to solve this puzzle. His cousin Pete, and their best friend Shelby (both also eleven) were with him every step of the way. So was an older man named Will Stoller, whose brother's name was on the western face of the monument. Dan reached out and touched the name carved into the reddish stone.

"Henry Stoller," Dan read. "What was it like to die so far from home? Did you know you weren't coming back?"

"I think he did," answered a voice from the other side of the monument. Dan jumped.

Will Stoller stepped into view. "Sorry," he apologized. "I didn't mean to startle you."

Will was in his seventies, but he could easily have passed for a man much younger. He had proven to be a good friend, and he was probably the one person in Freemont who truly understood why solving the mystery of the diary was so important to Dan.

Just as Will had waited for news of his brother to come home from a war so many years ago, Dan now waited to hear that his own father was coming home from a war. Dan's father flew fighter jets for the Navy and was stationed overseas in a very dangerous area.

"What happened to that boy's father and what happens with yours are not connected in any way. You know that, don't you?" Will looked kindly at Dan.

Dan knew it in his head, but he never quite felt it in his heart.

Will continued. "My brother's last letter to us felt like a good-bye. He told me to take care of my mother, that I could wear his jacket, that kind of thing. Has your father written you anything like that?"

Dan shook his head. His father had not. In fact, in his last letter he had continued with a subject that he and Dan had been writing back and forth about all summer.

It was a scripture passage, one of the few references to Jesus as a boy: *And Jesus grew in wisdom and stature and in favor with God and men.* Dan's father had asked Dan to give that verse some serious thought. Dan had, and different parts of it had jumped out at him over the past few months.

He had connected Jesus growing in wisdom to being smarter, growing in stature to growing stronger, and growing in favor with God to having a deeper relationship with his Heavenly Father. Dan knew that these were qualities that his own father expected him to develop as well. Now he was trying to figure out the last few words: what did growing in favor with men mean?

Well, thought Dan, hopefully it'll come to me if I think about it long enough. Another mystery of the universe solved by Daniel March Pruitt.

"Your mother invited me to come along with you tonight," Will told Dan. "Hope you don't mind."

Dan didn't mind at all. Will had become a part of his family. The old man had hidden himself away in his house for decades until a mistake (a mistake made by Dan, Pete, and Shelby) brought him out into the world again. Now Will was, as he put it, "making up for lost time."

He was seen everywhere in Freemont, usually being pulled from activity to activity by Dan's two younger sisters, Maureen and Eileen. The Eenies, as everyone called the girls, were only a year apart, and one was never seen without the other. They treated Will more like a younger brother than the dignified elderly gentleman he was.

Dan noticed Will staring off to a spot in the park to the North. He seemed concerned.

"Everything okay, Mr. Stoller?" Dan asked.

"I hope so," Will answered. Then, with a smile, he turned his attention to the names chiseled into the west side of the monument.

Dan and Will (and Shelby and Pete and the Eenies) had recently made a trip to a gathering of veterans of the Eighth Air Force in Washington, D.C. The boy who wrote the diary had drawn an elaborate picture of an airplane on one of the pages. It was a B-24, a bomber used by the American forces in Europe.

Because of that drawing, Dan and the others were fairly certain that the boy's father was part of the Eighth Air Force stationed in England. B-24's were an important part of "The Mighty Eighth," so off to Washington they went in search of information.

They'd met many interesting men, all with fascinating stories to tell. And they had narrowed down the possibilities of the boy's father to three names on the war memorial: Neil Murphy, Lloyd Parsifal, and Richard Jankowski. Their hopes were high when they returned to Freemont, but within a few days they had hit another dead end. Or rather, three dead ends.

None of the families of the three men were still in Freemont. In fact, there were no records on two of them after the war. Shelby was tracking down the Murphy family, but it was large and had split many times. It was like trying to find a specific strand of spaghetti on a very large plate of pasta.

"Do you think it would be smart to just stop searching?" Dan asked Will.

"Well, let's consider that," Will answered. "Have you found what you're hunting for yet? No. Are you closer? Hard to believe you're not. Have you learned anything along the way? If you haven't, you're not paying attention. Will you ever find out who wrote that diary? Not if you quit."

Dan laughed. But he quickly stopped when he spotted the same frown crease Will's face that was there a few moments before. Once again, Dan asked what was wrong.

"Don't turn around," Will ordered. "When I tell you to, I want you to look down toward the dock. There's a man there in a baseball hat. I want you to tell me if you've ever seen him before, but try not to let him catch you looking."

Eyes wide, Dan swallowed hard.

"Are we in danger?" he asked. Considering the events of the past summer, it was a logical question.

"Don't know," was the short answer. A few seconds later, Will told Dan to turn around.

Dan spotted a tall man with red hair and a Yankee's baseball hat. He *had* seen him before. Only . . .

"Turn back," Will said quickly. He pretended to study the names on the war memorial. Dan did, too.

"Now let's stroll toward the museum. Look casual," Will said.

They did. And as they did, it occurred to Dan that he had seen quite a bit of Will Stoller the past couple of days. He had shown up unexpectedly at the mall, the library, and even when Dan was walking home from visiting a friend. Suddenly Dan knew why. Just as he knew he had seen the red-haired man that morning—only then he'd had a beard.

"How long has that guy been stalking me?" Dan asked.

"Stalking may be taking it too far," Will replied.

"How long?" Dan insisted.

"A week."

PURSUIT

Neither Dan nor Will wanted to stop the family celebration at Cheezy World, the combination pizza parlor and video arcade that seemed to fascinate almost everyone under the age of twelve. Dan was not one of them that night, but he pretended to go along with the fun so he wouldn't ruin the party. The whole time they were there, he scanned the room for the man with the reddish hair. He never appeared. Dan didn't get the chance to talk to Will about it again, but when they all said goodnight, Will gave Dan a reassuring squeeze on the shoulder.

Dan woke up several times that night. And out of instinct he crossed and looked out his window. He thought it wasn't a coincidence that two of those times he spotted a police car cruise past the house. "Thanks for taking care of us, God," he whispered.

After such a restless night, Dan overslept the next morning. When his mother woke him for the third time, it was 7:32.

"Daniel Pruitt, your bus will be here in twenty minutes, and I can't drive you to school today. I have to get your grandfather to the doctor up in Pittsburgh. I have to leave in fifteen minutes. Now move!"

"Yes, ma'am," Dan said, yawning. The tests his grandfather was scheduled to take were very important and would keep him at the medical center overnight. "I'm up," he added through another yawn.

Dan pulled on his clothes, too tired to care that he was wearing one blue sock and one green. He then stumbled downstairs to say his good-byes as Grandpa Mike, his mother, and his brother, Jack, hurried to leave. The Eenies had taken an earlier bus to their school and were already gone.

"Ask me if I'm happy," Dan's mother ordered.

"Are you happy?"

"No."

"Sorry."

"Make sure you get on that bus," she said as she kissed Dan's forehead.

"I will."

Dan missed the bus.

It really wasn't his fault. The Eenies had tied the laces of his shoes together. By the time he unknotted them, the bus was roaring past his house.

"Would it have killed you to put on another pair of shoes instead, Pruitt?" he asked himself in a mocking tone.

Dan made a mental note to torture his sisters at the first possible opportunity, jumped on his bike, and headed for his school as fast as he could.

Brooks Hill Middle School was four and a half miles out of town on Old Route 10. It was uphill a lot of the way, but Dan figured that he could get there by the second bell and therefore wouldn't technically be tardy. When he realized this, Dan relaxed, and he set off in a better mood.

"Despite overwhelming odds, Pruitt races to retake the lead in the Tour de Freemont, trying to become the first person in over a hundred years to win the race wearing unmatched socks." In Dan's mind he was surrounded by an international pack of racers on bikes. "When reached for comment this morning, Mrs. Pruitt, Dan's supportive mother, had this to say . . . Dan then launched into a perfect imitation of his mother. "I'd like to point out that the socks, although mismatched, are clean."

Dan was soon out of town. The last house was behind him, and the only thing between him and the new middle school were fields. It was then that Dan noticed the car following him. A quick glance over his shoulder confirmed that *the man with the reddish hair was behind the wheel*.

Dan's first reaction was a stab of panic. He was out in the middle of nowhere. Panic, he knew, wouldn't do him any good.

"Okay, Pruitt, list your options," Dan said to himself.

Unfortunately, there weren't many options available to Dan. He could continue on and try to out-race him. He could abandon his bike and make a break for it across the fields. Or he could turn around and try and make it back into town, since town was closer than school.

Then, suddenly, coming over the hill a half-mile ahead, Dan saw an empty school bus returning to the garage after the morning run. Actually, it was the first of several, for if today was like every other day, they all would have left the middle school at the same time, which meant there was a line of about twelve busses coming Dan's way.

I have a shot, Dan thought. "I hope," he added aloud.

The maneuver would have to be executed with split second timing. If it backfired, it was going to mean another trip to the hospital. Or worse.

"Still, I have to try."

Another bus came over the hill, then another and another and another and . . .

"Good," whispered Dan. "Now just stay that way."

The first bus passed Dan. Then the second. There was about thirty feet or so between each vehicle. He made his move between the third and fourth bus.

Dan took a deep breath, turned sharply to the left, and cut in front of the bus. It all happened so quickly that the driver didn't even have time to slam on her brakes. In fact, from her lack of reaction, Dan wondered if she'd even seen him.

I'll worry about the quality of our bus drivers later, Dan thought. The important thing was that he was now going in the opposite direction. He was heading back into town, and, if he could pedal fast enough, he could use the school busses as a safety shield.

If. That was the problem. If Dan could keep pace with the busses. What if he fell behind? What if the busses made it into town before he did and he was out in the open again? The man might make a quick move and grab him.

Dan began to fall behind. He was even with the fifth bus, then the sixth, and then the seventh. There was still a quarter mile to go before the edge of town and his first chance to turn off and hide.

The eighth bus passed him. The ninth bus zipped by. There were only three busses to go, and then Dan would be at the mercy of his pursuer.

"For the honor of family, the flag, and disorganized young men with mismatched socks!" Dan shouted, trying to psych himself up.

Dan let loose with a burst of energy and pedaled with all his might. In seconds he was even with the ninth bus. Then he passed it. He gained on the eighth bus. He passed it. Franklin Street was just ahead on the right. If he could only keep up this level of effort . . .

The eighth bus passed Dan. He was falling behind again.

But he was almost to Franklin.

The ninth bus passed him.

Then, the corner! Dan took a sharp turn to the right, leapt off his bike, and hid behind a hedge.

Although panting and dripping with sweat, he had made it.

Through a space in the branches, Dan watched for the man with the reddish hair. Sure enough, soon after the last bus had passed, Dan saw him drive by in his little blue car.

"Take notes," Dan whispered to himself, meaning to study what he saw and try to remember as much of it as possible. He only had a few seconds to do this, for the hedge which concealed him also limited his view.

In addition to its color, Dan noticed that the car was a new model. It had an out of state license plate, and he caught an "L" and maybe a "5" on the plate. The man with the reddish hair searched to the left and right for some sign of Dan.

Dan waited another ten minutes. As he did, a familiar yowl and a gray patch of fur told him that his cousin Pete's insane cat, Chester, was in the hedge with him.

Chester was a legend in Freemont, and he roamed the streets unafraid. When people saw him coming, they actually ran inside and locked their doors. Dogs, big ones, ran for cover. Several of them were missing ears, and at least one was without a tail because of Chester. The only word for him was fierce.

Dan relaxed. If Chester were going to strike, it would have already happened. Dan would be lying bruised and bloody and probably in much worse shape than if the red-haired man had caught up with him. As it was, Chester rubbed up against him as if to say hello, and then took off after a bird.

Dan hopped back on his bike. Using every possible side street and concealed alley, he raced to the police station.

An hour later, Dan studied the finished picture that the police artist had drawn from Dan's description.

"That's him," Dan said with a nod. "And yesterday he had a beard."

The sketch artist photocopied the picture, then following Dan's instructions, added a beard.

"That's him, too," Dan stated with confidence.

Dan watched as the sketches were scanned into the computer and distributed to all the police in the area.

Dan called his mother to explain what had happened. He tried to keep the conversation private, but he was sure several of the officers were laughing when he told her that he had missed the bus because the Eenies had sabotaged his sneakers. It was decided that the police would drive Dan to school.

"All things considered, I think it's the safest place for you," Sergeant Haines said.

For obvious reasons, Dan was well known, even though this was his first year in Freemont. To his credit, he tried to play his celebrity status down. Dan knew better than most the pitfalls of being famous. Finding favor did not give him the right to exploit his popularity.

Which is why, when he came over the crest of the hill in the police car and saw that his entire school was assembled outside because of a fire drill, Dan cringed. "I need to be the center of attention again like a cow needs a bottle of ketchup."

Sergeant Haines seemed to find it all very funny.

"Shall I turn on the lights and siren and make it a big entrance?" he asked.

"No!" shouted Dan. Then, calmer, he added, "I mean, please, I'd rather you didn't."

Dan got out of the car to a few hoots from some of the eighth-graders, but mostly his fellow students just stared in amazement.

Okay, Pruitt, try and make this seem as normal as possible, he told himself.

Normal? Who comes to school in a police car?

Maybe if you make a joke . . .

"And next time, *you* pay for the doughnuts," Dan said to Sergeant Haines before shutting the door. He then banged twice on the roof as a signal for him to take off. Which he did—with lights flashing and siren blasting. Dan cringed again.

By mid-morning it was all over the school that Dan Pruitt had solved a murder, prevented a bank robbery, and had a part-time job with the police force for which he was getting extra credit in Social Studies.

Shelby and Pete finally caught up with Dan during lunch.

"Very smooth this morning, Dan," Shelby said with a straight face. "I wasn't sure you'd made enough of a name for yourself around here. Now I think people finally know who you are."

"Sarah Conners sat next to me in art," Pete added, "and spent twenty-seven solid minutes talking about you."

"I think you can pretty much count on the Most Popular Guy in Class Award at the end of the year."

"This isn't popularity," Dan insisted. "This is . . ."

"Love?"

"Adoration?"

"Curiosity," Dan answered. "I'm like the two-headed snake at the zoo."

Shelby studied him. "I can see the resemblance."

After school Dan, Shelby, and Pete went to Eckert House so Miss Alma could keep an eye on Dan. They saw a well-dressed man sitting patiently in one of the large chairs in the entrance hall. He was reading a book and looked so settled and comfortable that he might have been part of an exhibit.

Mrs. Doheny was once again back at her post, greeting visitors from behind a small desk. As they passed her, she put her finger to her lips. The way she looked at the man in the chair made it clear that he was the reason for their silence.

Shelby paused on the second floor to glance back down the staircase at the stranger.

"That is a handsome man," she whispered. "How old do you think he is?"

"Why? You want to date him?"

Shelby slugged Dan in the arm. Hard.

"Ouch!" he cried.

"Shhh!" hissed Mrs. Doheny from below.

Shelby gave Pete and Dan a shove, and they continued up the stairs to the third floor.

"Shall I go back down and ask him if he's busy tonight?" Dan asked Shelby.

"Why don't you do that," she agreed. "And then keep on walking. Don't stop—even when you get to the river."

When they arrived at Miss Alma's office, she wasn't there. They went in to wait.

"First of all, that guy down there couldn't be any more than twenty-eight or twenty-nine. Now, put that together with the fact that his ring has a ruby in it the size of a baseball, his shoes don't look like they've ever touched the ground, that haircut had to cost him more than most people earn in a week, and his clothes looked like they were sewn right onto him, and what do you have?"

Dan and Pete were at a loss.

"I'd say you have someone who didn't spend a lot of his time waiting for anything or anyone. And yet there he is down there just as calm as can be."

"You saw all that just by walking by him?" Dan was amazed.

"Yes, Mr. Popularity, and you might have seen it too if you hadn't been so busy looking at your own reflection in the mirror."

Dan felt a little foolish. Not because of Shelby's remark. Considering how messy his hair usually was, and how rumpled his clothes often were, looking in a mirror was something he knew he really should do more often. No, it was more serious than that. Here someone had been following him, maybe for days, and he hadn't been paying any attention. Dan knew that kind of carelessness could get him into serious trouble.

"So who do you think he is?" Pete asked.

Miss Alma appeared in the doorway. "His name is Rainer Leopold. His official title is Prince of Penrod-Holtz. He is well educated, very rich, undeniably handsome, and a royal pain in the neck. I've been avoiding him for days, but he won't go away."

"Why would you want him to?" Shelby asked before she could stop herself. She then whacked Dan on the arm before he could say anything. Miss Alma's answer was troubling.

"He says we have something of his."

"Tell him we'd be glad to let him have Shelby as long as he promises he won't try to exchange her later," quipped Dan. This time Dan thought Miss Alma might take a swing at him. The look on her face was one of cold fury.

"This is not funny, Mr. Pruitt. This museum, as we now know, contains works of art that are worth a great deal of money—not to mention their historic value. If the Eckerts obtained any of them by less than honest means, we could lose everything. We might also be involved in an international scandal."

Dan's smile was long gone. "What is it that he says we have?" he asked.

"That's just it. He won't tell me."

CONNECTIONS

Miss Alma phoned down to Mrs. Doheny and asked her to send the man upstairs.

"What do we call him?" asked Dan.

"Mr. Leopold will do just fine," Miss Alma answered.

There wasn't a soul on earth who intimidated Miss Alma, and she had no use for royalty. Besides,

Penrod-Holtz wasn't really a country; it was a duchy. A duchy, she explained, was a territory ruled by a duke or a prince. Technically Penrod-Holtz was just a small part of Germany. Although Rainer Leopold was a real prince, he didn't rule the duchy. There was a local government for that.

"He's just there for decoration," she said in a disapproving tone.

There was a light tap on the door. He was there.

Dan's first impression of "Mr. Leopold" was that he looked like a movie star. Tall, tan, and trim. He wore a dark gray suit, a pale blue shirt, and an orange and black-striped tie. His shoes practically gleamed, and as Shelby had already observed, the ring on his right hand featured an enormous ruby. The only thing that seemed to be out of place was a tie clip in the shape of a tiger. Dan felt like a slob. He took a step backward.

"Good afternoon, Miss Stockton LeMay," the man said in a clipped accent. It didn't sound American *or* European.

"Good afternoon," Miss Alma replied. She then introduced Dan, Shelby, and Pete. "How long have you been waiting?"

"Four hours and twenty-seven minutes," he answered without a trace of anger. He held up his hand. On his wrist was an expensive-looking watch. "I took your advice."

"Isn't that wonderful," Miss Alma replied.

Dan was peering at the man's face. "Is that your real nose?" he asked innocently.

"Daniel Pruitt!" Miss Alma exclaimed.

"Oh, c'mon, Miss Alma, you can't deny that it looks just like what's his name's nose. You know, that movie star." Dan turned back to the man. "Do you have the same plastic surgeon?"

The answer was no.

"You use a different doctor?"

The man laughed and promised he didn't, that his nose was untouched. "There is a castle in Europe, and if you go there and look at the portraits of my ancestors, you can see that this nose can be found on all of them, going back hundreds of years."

"So what happens? Do they take it off and pass it on just before they die?"

Shelby interrupted before Miss Alma could pounce.

"So what do you like to be called?"

"My friends call me Rain," he answered, "which is short for Rainer. If you want to be more formal, you can say Prince Rainer. Or more formal still, Prince Rainer Leopold the Fourth of Penrod-Holtz. Miss Stockton Lemay calls me Mr. Leopold, which isn't technically correct but perfectly acceptable. Then again, everything in this country seems to be acceptable."

Rainer smiled at Miss Alma as he said this, but Dan could tell he was trying to make a serious point.

Miss Alma smiled coolly at him.

"So what is it you do exactly?" Shelby wanted to know.

"I wait," he answered.

"Nice work if you can get it," Dan commented.

"Some things are worth waiting for," Rainer answered. He then turned to Miss Alma. "Well, Miss Stockton Lemay, what's it to be? Will you allow me to look at your records here in Eckert House?"

The answer was a definite no, but she was going to allow Dan, Pete, and Shelby to escort him around the museum. He could look at some of the rooms and artifacts that the public did not normally see. "Take it or leave it, Mr. Leopold."

He took it. An hour later Dan, Pete, and Shelby returned to Miss Alma's office to report what had happened.

"How does a human being get to smell that good?" Shelby wondered.

"Did you notice how he seemed to know more about the Eckerts than we did?" Pete pointed out.

"How come his hair never moved?" Dan said, amazed.

But none of these questions were why Miss Alma had sent them off with Prince Rainer Leopold the Fourth of Penrod-Holtz. She wanted to know what he had been interested in, what questions he had asked, where he had wanted to go. All of that was easy: he was interested in the north and south wings of Eckert House.

Eckert House had originally been built in the 1860s, and the north and south wings were added in the late 1870s. The entire structure, both the main part of the house and the additions, had secret passageways, hidden staircases, and concealed rooms.

Over the summer, Dan had experienced many of them firsthand—and not always in a pleasant way. Any desires he once had to explore the unexplored spaces inside the mansion were long gone. But it was just those hidden places that Rainer Leopold seemed to ask about. He didn't say anything directly, but he'd heard rumors that there was a lot more to Eckert House than met the eye.

"We didn't say anything," Dan assured Miss Alma.

There was one room in particular that interested Rainer. It was the Music Room in the north wing. It was not usually open to the public because it was covered with mirrors. The mirrors were brought to America from France and dated all the way back to the 1700s. They were very valuable.

"He searched every corner of that room," Pete reported. "He said something about the mirrors in one of his castles."

"He was also interested in the Garden Room in the south wing," Shelby added.

The Garden Room wasn't a garden, but a room decorated like one that the Eckerts had used for afternoon teas. The Eckerts were known for their parties, and over the years many famous people had visited the mansion. The walls of the room were covered with rare Chinese silk.

Dan thought it was odd that Rainer spent so much time in both the Music Room and the Garden Room. "Other than the mirrors and the silk wallpaper, there's not much in either of them that should interest—" Dan stopped.

"What?" asked Shelby. She studied Dan's face, waiting.

"Does it strike anybody as odd that there are only two rooms in Eckert House that are exactly the same size, and that this Rainer guy was interested in both of them?"

It did. And as Dan thought about the time spent with him, it almost seemed like he was measuring both rooms and just trying not to be obvious about it.

They all went downstairs and inspected the two rooms.

"What does he want?" Dan wondered out loud, not really expecting an answer.

"Who does he think he is?" growled Miss Alma, not expecting a response either.

But it was a question that sparked Shelby's interest. "Miss Alma, just what exactly do you know about this man?"

A few minutes later, Shelby, Dan, and Pete were all seated on the floor in Miss Alma's office. They studied a file of pages Miss Alma had printed off the Internet about Prince Rainer Leopold the Fourth of Penrod-Holtz. It contained the usual information such as place and date of birth, parents, extended family, royal titles, and ties to other royal families.

There were several articles about his romance and engagement to a French actress, and other articles about his travels.

"Everywhere this guy goes, he gets his picture taken," Dan remarked.

There were photos of Rainer Leopold in castles, country houses, churches, town halls, parks, and theaters. His main interest was the preservation of ancient buildings. All the pictures were from European magazines and newspapers.

Dan thought it was a bit much. "What is it with all their interest in royalty? He's just a guy like the rest of us."

He then held up one photo spread in particular. It was after Rainer had broken up with the actress. Half the page showed him with the ex-girlfriend, and the other showed him looking sadly at a sixteenth century statue in Italy that resembled her. There was a caption in German they didn't understand.

Miss Alma translated. "It says 'What is Rainer Really Looking For?'" She made a snort of disapproval. "Indeed."

The journalist who wrote the article had written several others as well. His name was Jurgen Glick, and it looked like he had made a career of following and writing about Prince Rainer Leopold. Dan held up the most recent article from a German tabloid. He asked Miss Alma to translate.

"He keeps using a phrase that roughly means 'looking for his golden moment and missing it.' That's odd. Other than that, it's the usual silliness about heartbreak and true love and a prince in search of his princess." Miss Alma lowered the page. "It's depressing enough that people read this nonsense, but that someone gets paid to write it boggles the mind."

When Miss Alma finished showing them the pages she had printed about the prince, Shelby asked if she could sit at the computer and give it a try herself. Shelby was so good at finding information on the Internet that Dan had nicknamed her Search Engine. It was a nickname she hated, but one that was fitting. It seemed that, given enough time, there was no information Shelby could not find out. Miss Alma was more than happy to let Shelby do it. Shelby got lucky very quickly.

"Miss Alma," she asked casually, "did you know that the duchy of Penrod-Holtz used to be three very small countries?"

Miss Alma did not.

"One was called Norvania. And although it was small, it had a pretty solid army that it used to hire out to other countries."

Miss Alma did not know this either, although she certainly knew about the practice of one country hiring another country's army.

"Back in 1691, Peter the Great of Russia was having some trouble with—"

"Mercy!" Miss Alma exclaimed, cutting Shelby off. "Rainer Leopold is a descendent of King Wilhelm III of Norvania!" She sat down in the nearest chair. "No, it couldn't be. It's just not possible."

Dan had never seen Miss Alma this upset. He looked at Shelby, who was still at the computer. "What's this all about?" he whispered.

Shelby motioned for him to come to the computer.

"The Golden Room," he read. "What's that?"

It was, he soon learned, the most famous lost piece of art in the world. And Prince Rainer Leopold the Fourth of Penrod-Holtz thought it was right there in Eckert House.

HISTORY

"Okay, what do we know, and what are we just guessing at?" Dan asked.

The facts that Dan, Pete, Shelby, and Miss Alma had gathered over the previous twenty-four hours were varied. They shared them with each other at the kitchen table in Eckert House as they munched popcorn.

Fact: In 1650, a Russian monk named Vladamir the Meek had a dream in which he was standing in a golden room. He felt it was a glimpse of the glory of heaven and saw it as a sign from God to construct such a room so that others could experience this as well. However, being a penniless monk, Vladamir had no way to make this happen. So he set out on a thousand-mile journey—on foot—to convince a Russian nobleman to build the golden room. He was successful.

"That must have been some sales pitch," said Dan.

Fact: In 1660, the Golden Room was completed and installed in the nobleman's estate. By every written account (and there were many) it was one of the wonders of the world. Everything was made of gold: walls, ceiling, furniture—everything. One of the walls was sculpted into a mountain scene, another like the ocean, the third like clouds in the sky, and the last like fire. The ceiling portrayed the sun, the moon, and the stars. When sunlight hit the walls, the reflection was so bright that people had to cover their eyes. At night, with hundreds of candles lit, it was said the walls themselves glowed. All accounts of the Golden Room called it nothing less than a miracle.

Shelby held up a piece of paper. "This historian reports that many people actually fainted when they saw it."

Fact: By 1675, only those who lived on the estate were allowed to see the Golden Room. There had simply been too many problems with strangers showing up and demanding to be let into the castle.

"I guess it would have been pretty hard to call ahead," Pete offered.

Fact: In 1691, Peter the Great, Czar of Russia, was fighting a series of wars and needed help from another army. He made a deal with King Wilhelm III of Norvania: send me your soldiers and I will send you the Golden Room as payment. An agreement was made, Peter the Great won his war, and Lichtenburgh Castle in Norvania became the new home of the Golden Room.

"All in all, not a bad deal," Dan observed.

Fact: The trade was rumored but wasn't proven until 1787 when the Prince of Penrod-Holtz defeated Norvania in a minor war. Norvania became a part of Penrod-Holtz. When the prince inspected Lichtenburgh Castle, he discovered the Golden Room. The general public was not allowed to see it, but a few famous people, like Beethoven, were given permission.

"Some music scholars even think one of Beethoven's sonatas is a tribute to the Golden Room," Miss Alma added.

Fact: The Golden Room was photographed in 1853. Even the black and white images of it were beautiful.

"Were there ever any color pictures taken of it?" Dan asked. There were not.

Fact: During World War Two, the Nazis seized Lichtenburgh Castle and used it as a military headquarters. When it appeared Germany was losing the war, a number of trucks pulled up to the castle, and the Nazis drove away with everything of value inside.

"That's what we know for sure," said Dan. "Here's where it gets tricky." There were several stories about what may, or may not, have happened to the Golden Room. Since it was worth millions, many were interested in finding it. There were three possible explanations.

"Story number one," began Dan. The convoy of trucks that pulled away from Lichtenburgh Castle contained crates into which the disassembled Golden Room was packed. The trucks were bombed as they approached Munich. When the smoke cleared, what little was left inside was stolen by the people who lived nearby. "Pretty grim," Dan commented. *Supposed* proof of this story was a little golden star that turned up many years after the end of the war. It was said to be from the ceiling of the Golden Room, and was found in a home near where the trucks had been destroyed in 1945.

"Which brings us to story number two." The same convoy of trucks drove the crates high into the Alps and dumped them into a lake. The plan was to recover the treasure after the war was over. "But," Dan continued, "American bombers make an appearance in this version, too." On the way back, planes supposedly hit the German trucks, and everyone who knew which lake contained the Golden Room was killed. "Again, not a happy ending," Dan added. "But a German diving crew claims to have found evidence of large man-made objects — possibly crates — at the bottom of a lake in the Alps. The problem is, the lake, in addition to being very, very deep, is on the border of Austria and Germany. There's a big argument about who has a right to whatever's down there." Dan also pointed out that it could be anything at all in the water, from a wrecked airplane to a sunken boat.

"Story number three is less dramatic but maybe makes the most sense." Dan explained that the last of the widely circulated stories about the Golden Room was that the Russians knew that it was in Lichtenburgh Castle, got to it before the Nazis could move it, and took it back to Russia where they felt it truly belonged.

"The Russians did not feel they owed anybody an explanation since it was really theirs anyway, and that was that," Dan reported. "Oh, except that there were a couple of Americans who claim that, during a party in 1955, a Russian general took them deep into the basement of the Kremlin and showed it to them."

"Could that be true?" Pete wondered.

They agreed that, with something as mysterious as the Golden Room, anything was possible. One of the people who saw it was the brother of a US Senator.

"And what do you think, Mr. Pruitt?" Miss Alma asked.

Dan was prepared for this question. "I think it's strange that, for something so famous, there's no actual proof that it's been seen since 1853. Stories, yeah, but if you read the reports carefully, no one actually mentions that it was there."

"I was hoping you'd pick up on that. Very good." Miss Alma nodded. "This brings us to Julius Eckert's travel diary." Miss Alma took the volumes Dan had gotten out of the safe and opened one of them. "In 1868, Julius Eckert traveled to Europe. According to his diary, he never went anywhere near Lichten-burgh Castle. In fact, he goes out of his way to write that he was *not* in that part of Europe."

Dan frowned. "How did he do that?"

"By writing that he tried to meet a distant cousin there and couldn't because of the flooding. Which is interesting since they were in the middle of a drought." Miss Alma grinned at Shelby. "You taught me a thing or two about surfing the Web yesterday."

Miss Alma, it turned out, had done quite a bit of surfing.

"I have noticed," Miss Alma said, "that people like Julius Eckert, who keep very detailed records and notes, can't, because of their personalities, keep from sharing the truth at least somewhere in their writing. You keep a diary in the first place because you want to put down the truth in black and white."

Dan thought of the boy who wrote the diary during World War Two. He had shared some very real feelings about his fears; he wanted the truth on paper.

"So why did Julius Eckert lie about going to Lichtenburgh Castle? And despite that, how did he manage to get the truth into his travel diary about his visit?" Miss Alma showed them a passage in which Julius Eckert wrote about meeting a composer in Vienna who was working on an idea for an opera, a story from the Old Testament. The composer was not named.

"Julius Eckert writes that he gave a very large sum of money to a composer to finish the opera. I checked the other records. In 1868, money was transferred from the Eckert account in the US to a bank in Vienna."

"How much?"

"One hundred thousand dollars — with the promise of twenty thousand more."

Dan was stunned. He knew that would equal several million dollars today. "For an *opera*?" he finally said.

"I don't think any of us believe that the money went to pay for an opera," Miss Alma said.

"But why do you think it went to buy the Golden Room?" was the obvious question.

"Because Julius Eckert tells us so in a clever way."

Miss Alma showed them a page written by Julius Eckert. It contained several lines of music, supposedly one of the main themes from the opera on which the composer was working. Beneath it Julius Eckert had written a few comments about the high quality of the music and that he was sure his investment was solid. *With this festive march, I will take my place in history,* he concluded.

"This music is never identified. But I called a friend who's an expert on opera and told her what I was looking for. Her answer convinced me that this is a reference to the Golden Room. The music is from *The Queen of Sheba,* an opera based on a theme from the Old Testament. The Queen of Sheba had a reputation for riches and wealth beyond counting. That in itself is Julius Eckert winking at us. But the fact that the opera was written by Carl *Gold*mark, in my opinion, seals the fact that he purchased the Golden Room from its owners for one hundred twenty thousand dollars. Which is interesting when you consider the Queen of Sheba gave Solomon one hundred twenty talents of gold. Julius Eckert couldn't help but boast about what he'd done, and he put it all in here in code."

Dan had a question. "Why did Rainer Leopold's ancestors sell the Golden Room?"

It was sold for the same reason all such things are sold: they needed the money. "Being royal and being rich do not always go together," Miss Alma informed them. As for how the room was shipped to America . . . Miss Alma produced another document. "The mirrors that cover the walls of the Music

Room arrived in 1872. In fifty large crates. Now I'm all for careful packing, but—"

"It was really the Golden Room! Those mirrors didn't need all that space!" exclaimed Dan. He ran out of the kitchen.

A few moments later, Miss Alma, Shelby, and Pete caught up with Dan in the Music Room.

"This room is forty feet by twenty feet," Dan shouted. "Those are the dimensions of the Golden Room. It's here! It's under these mirrors. It has to be!"

MISTAKES

It took Miss Alma a minute to quiet Dan down.

"May I remind you, Mr. Pruitt, that this museum is open for business. The way you're carrying on, anybody can hear you!"

Dan realized Miss Alma was right. Lately Rainer Leopold had been in Eckert House whenever it was open. Although Dan had not seen him when he ran from the kitchen to the Music Room, it didn't mean he wasn't around.

"Sorry," Dan whispered.

Pete's dad (Dan's Uncle Jeff) looked in on them. He was the head of security for the museum. "Are we okay in here?" he asked.

"Are we, Mr. Pruitt?" Miss Alma asked with an edge in her voice.

Dan assured her that they were.

They decided that nothing could be done until the weekend.

The following Saturday they were ready to start. The museum was closed early, and to keep Rainer Leopold from getting suspicious, Miss Alma had a plumbing truck parked outside. They never spotted Rainer, but Miss Alma was sure he was watching.

What Miss Alma didn't know was that Dan had also put some of his buddies on the case. Jesse and Dylan Crane, the twins known as the Raccoon Brothers because of all the trouble they caused, and Ted Jamison, a quiet kid who was a fearless dare-devil, were circling the block and patrolling the park in what looked like a game of contact tag. Their real purpose was keeping an eye out for Rainer Leopold and the man with the red hair. Dan didn't explain why he needed their help, only that he did. They were glad to cause as much confusion as possible.

"It's what we do," Jesse said simply.

An odd thing had happened since the day Dan arrived at school in the police car. The interest in him, the "freak factor" as Dan called it, had given way to something else: a kind of respect. This was in part because the real story got out.

The other part was because of a letter Dan had written in the school paper. Dan wrote about wanting to be liked for who you are, not just for the things you do. To his surprise, his classmates understood what he meant.

True popularity, Dan realized, was not how people reacted to you in the middle of all the excitement. It had more to do with how they felt about you afterward, when everything settled down and life got back to normal. It was about things like whether they could count on you to be a regular guy, whether they saw Jesus in your actions.

Real popularity was more than just hitting the home run or winning the award or being all over the news. It was a go-the-distance thing, not a sprint.

Cooler, Dan had written to his father, *is being liked for who you really are.*

Dan's friends picked up on this, which was why, he thought, they were willing to help. He didn't give them details; he just said he needed them, and they came through.

Dan smiled as he looked out across the park to where Dylan and Ted were pretending to beat Jesse with a plastic bat.

"Whenever you're ready, Mr. Pruitt," Miss Alma said impatiently. Dan turned and headed to the north wing.

There were three tall windows in the Music Room, all facing west, and their drapes were usually closed to protect the antique mirrors. They were closed now to keep prying eyes from peering in at them.

The plan was to carefully remove one of the smaller mirrors. They would then remove whatever was beneath it since they didn't think the mirrors would be attached right to the gold itself. Uncle Jeff had worked for a builder once and was sure he could remove the mirror without damaging it.

"Just remember, Mr. March," Miss Alma said as he slowly worked around the edges of the first mirror to remove, "that little section is worth thousands of dollars."

"No pressure, though, right?" he shot back with a smile.

No matter what Miss Alma said or did, Dan noticed it never seemed to upset his uncle. After an hour's worth of cautious loosening (with Dan and

Pete holding the mirror in place), Uncle Jeff grabbed the handles of the two large suction cups already attached to the surface of the glass. Ever so slowly, he pulled. The mirror came off the wall. They laid it on a blanket already spread out on the floor and turned to study the wall. It was covered with very thick plaster. Everyone moved up close to see if there was any sign of another wall beneath it.

Miss Alma held a small tool with a very sharp point. She also had a soft brush. "If you don't mind," she said. Everyone backed away. After examining the wall with a magnifying glass, she chose a spot and picked the plaster away bit by bit. She used the brush to remove any dust.

Uncle Jeff was unclear as to why Julius Eckert would buy something as valuable as the Golden Room and then hide it.

"Because," explained Miss Alma as she worked, "he didn't pay for all of it. He still owed the Leopold family twenty thousand dollars. There's no record of it ever being paid. Which is why Mr. Leopold thinks it's still his." It was Miss Alma's belief that Julius Eckert planned to uncover the walls soon after the man he bought it from died. But Julius Eckert died first.

Dan felt there was a simpler explanation. "The guy had a screw loose."

"There's something under here," Miss Alma announced.

Once again they all crowded around the spot on the wall. To Dan it looked like a sculpted body of some kind. Miss Alma took a cleaning solution and gently dabbed the area. It *was* a body . . . a man. There were wings on his feet. It looked to be made out of metal!

Miss Alma stopped cleaning and stepped away. "This isn't it," she said. "No use going any further."

"What?" Dan couldn't believe what he was hearing. "Why not?"

"Look closely at the figure, particularly the feet. That's Hermes," she explained, "a figure from Greek mythology. The Golden Room is full of Christian imagery. Whatever this is, it's not what we're looking for. A Russian monk would not have had a vision of a Greek god."

Dan could tell that the others were as disappointed as he was. However, unlike the others, Dan could not just stand there.

"If the Golden Room isn't here, there's only one place it can be." He headed to the Garden Room and started running his hands along the walls. "The mirrors in the other room were only put there to make us think the Golden Room was underneath. It was a trick. It must be here."

Everyone, including Miss Alma, had followed Dan. "So now I'm supposed to tear apart another wall in this museum?" Miss Alma was not happy.

"Do you honestly think the Golden Room isn't somewhere in this house?"

Miss Alma stared at Dan for a long time. She marched over to the corner. She spent a minute studying how the seams of the wallpaper met in the corner.

"This wallpaper is made of expensive silk," she said simply.

"The baseboard isn't," Dan pointed out.

Half an hour later, a section of the fancy baseboard along the floor had been pulled away from the wall. There was nothing underneath it. The Golden Room was not in this room either.

"We're not wrong," Dan said. "I can feel it. It's here somewhere. Not in this room, but somewhere." Dan knew that his enthusiasm was all they had, and that he had to somehow keep them going. "I'm going to find it," he declared.

Before anyone could respond, there was a furious knocking on the front door. Dan's uncle took charge.

It was Mrs. O'Hara. The O'Haras lived in the house nearest to the museum. It was the first house to the south, just across Filkins Street. Like Eckert House, it too faced the park and the river.

Relations between the O'Haras and Eckert House had been just fine until Dan Pruitt came along. Then, according to Mrs. O'Hara, Dan had set into motion a series of events that had brought thugs, burglars, art thieves, kidnappers, and murderers to the neighborhood. While Dan couldn't deny that technically this was true, he didn't feel he should be held responsible for the criminal choices of others.

Nevertheless, a "For Sale" sign had gone up in front of the O'Hara house just after Rick Doheny was captured by the FBI. The arrest had taken place at the war memorial across the street, only yards from Mrs. O'Hara's front door.

Uncle Jeff let Mrs. O'Hara in.

"You!" she shouted, pointing a finger at Dan.

Dan could honestly not think of a single thing he'd done wrong. Mrs. O'Hara soon set him straight. It seemed that Jesse's, Dylan's, and Ted's little game of contact tag had spilled over into a hedge where a strange man was hiding. And a cat. Chester.

They stopped pretending to beat each other up and proceeded to attack the man for real. He fled for his life. Chester got into the act and chased Jesse and Dylan.

Mrs. O'Hara's doors were wide open because her carpets were being cleaned, and the man, the boys, and the cat ran up the front stairs, down the back stairs, out through the yard, and over the back fence.

"And I know you're involved! They shouted something about some man with red hair who was after you," she screamed at Dan.

As soon as Mrs. O'Hara mentioned the man with the red hair, Uncle Jeff whipped out his cell phone. He was calling the police as he ran out the front door. Miss Alma kept Dan, Pete, and Shelby from following, which meant they had to listen to Mrs. O'Hara yell at Dan some more.

"The happiest day of my life will be when that moving van pulls up out front and I'm on my way back to Oklahoma. At least there I'll be able to run to the storm cellar when a tornado is coming. With you here in Freemont, there's no place to hide!"

That's when it hit Dan. That's when he realized their mistake. Dan couldn't help it. He gave Mrs. O'Hara a big hug. A moment later she ran out of Eckert House. Miss Alma just glared at him.

"Sorry," Dan mumbled. He stared at the floor, not because he was embarrassed, but because he was sure he knew where the Golden Room was and he didn't want to give it away. He felt partly responsible for the mistakes that had already been made. This time, before he revealed anything, he wanted to be one hundred percent sure.

Patience, Pruitt, Dan told himself. It's been hidden and forgotten for over a hundred years. It's not going anywhere.

DISCOVERY

Dan was escorted home by Miss Alma. Pete tagged along since his father was still with the police. They were ordered to stay put.

So Pete and Dan went to spend time with their Grandpa Mike. Grandpa Mike loved having the Bible and the sports pages read to him. Dan and Pete took turns.

Will Stoller was also with them tonight, as he often was. Although Mr. Stoller and Grandpa Mike hadn't known each other very well as boys (Will Stoller was older by a few years), as Mr. Stoller often said, "It's never too late to make a new old friend."

Will Stoller was turning out to be a good friend to Dan and his family in a lot of ways. Dan's mom had asked Will to stay with Grandpa Mike while she helped supervise the Eenies on their Scout troop's campout in a few weeks.

Will had a better idea. Since Grandpa Mike had two doctors' appointments in Pittsburgh that week, and since they had already talked of attending a football game, Will suggested they make a week of it.

Because of the stroke, Grandpa Mike had trouble speaking, but Dan noticed that no matter how long it took Grandpa Mike to finish a sentence, Will Stoller never seemed impatient. Dan often finished his grandfather's sentences for him—something he knew didn't always make his grandfather happy. Dan and Pete left Will and their grandfather talking about some of the great Pittsburgh Pirates teams of the past.

As it often did when they were together, Dan and Pete's conversation turned to the World War Two diary. It lay on Dan's desk. Pete opened to the page with a clue that they had misinterpreted. It was a music staff with several notes on it. The time signature (the symbol that indicated the rhythm at which the music should be played) was a "2" over a "4."

This "clue" had mistakenly led them to Will Stoller. While that was good, Dan now thought that the notes were random and not a clue at all. "Although I have to admit, seeing that music written in Julius Eckert's diary made me wonder again . . ."

Pete was still convinced the music in the diary meant something. He hummed and tapped out the strange two-note tune the notes represented. "Weird," he muttered, for the quarter note followed by the triplet followed by the quarter notes just didn't make musical sense all by itself.

Dan turned the diary pages to where the boy had drawn pictures of several cartoon characters. He stopped at one. "By the way, I checked, and this really is Woody Woodpecker. In the early 40s, he had a long sharp beak and his head feathers stood up more. The cartoonist changed him later." The boys then studied the detailed drawing of the B-24, the plane they believed the boy's father flew during the war. Dan's thoughts went to the names of the men on the monument in the park.

He was glad his grandfather was speaking more now, for Dan hoped to ask him about some of the families in Freemont back in the 40s. The problem was, Grandpa Mike didn't like to talk about his childhood.

Before the stroke he loved to ask riddles and tell funny stories and play games, but he always changed the subject when asked about his boyhood.

An hour later, Dan's mother stuck her head in the door to announce that Pete's father was there to pick Pete up.

First, Uncle Jeff had some news. He said the red-haired man had vanished without a trace. Dan's buddies were interviewed by the police, and the results were odd. Each of them felt the sketch made by the police artist from Dan's earlier description was wrong. Each, in turn, sat with the same sketch artist. Each came up with a completely different picture. Jesse's looked like the school principal, Dylan's looked like Jesse, and Ted's looked exactly like the man who was making the drawing. Dan shook his head at the news.

After Pete left with his dad, Dan hunted for his mom and found her in the kitchen. "Mom, when did Grandpa Mike's father die? It was right after World War Two, wasn't it?"

"Yes. 1947. A car accident."

"Did he ever talk about his father when you were little?"

"No. I think it was just too sad. He was only a teenager when it happened. He had to drop out of high school and go right to work to support his family."

"To get all the way through a war just to come home and die . . ." Dan's voice trailed off. He was thinking of his own father.

His mother moved to give him a hug. "There's a small box of my grandfather's belongings up in the attic. I don't know what's in it, but it might be interesting. And you never know, Grandpa Mike may be willing to talk about it now."

"Couldn't hurt," Dan agreed.

That night, as he lay in bed, Dan went over the events of the day: the reappearance of the red-haired man, the absence of Rainer Leopold, the disappointments in the Music Room and the Garden Room, Mrs. O'Hara, and even his discussion with Pete about the diary.

It was the Golden Room that got him out of bed. "The Golden Room." Dan sat at his desk with a piece of paper, a pencil, and a ruler. He drew the floor plans to Eckert House to the best of his ability — including all the secret passages, concealed stairways, and hidden rooms. After studying the layout for half an hour, he was pretty sure he knew where to hunt for the Golden Room.

"Let me know if I'm getting off track here," he said aloud in prayer. The next day, Sunday, brought a discovery of a different kind, one regarding Rainer Leopold and the red-haired man. After church, Shelby stopped by to keep Dan company. Since Shelby was something of a football nut, and since the season was in full swing, they naturally watched the game.

It was during one of the frequent sports updates that it happened. Dan didn't follow college football at all, but Shelby did—especially the University of Notre Dame. Because of the events of the day before, she'd missed the game and even forgot to check on the score. When the college recap came on, she paid close attention.

One game that received a lot of coverage involved an Ivy League school, Regency, better known for its academics and Nobel Prize winners than for its sports teams. This year, though, they had a football team that was undefeated. There was even talk that they would go to a bowl game. All that was fine, but it was the school mascot and the school colors that caught Dan's eye. The colors were orange and black. The mascot was a tiger.

"Regency University!" Dan yelled. He ran to the computer. "Help me," he called out. Shelby did, and their search produced three solid facts.

1. Regency's mascot was a tiger, the same tiger that appeared on Rainer Leopold's tie clip.
2. Prince Rainer Leopold went to Regency. His biographical information had only said an Ivy League education. A close examination of the class list from six years ago produced his name. Dan remembered the black-and-orange striped tie he wore the first day they met him: Regency's colors.
3. The red-haired man was featured in a photograph standing next to the prince. His name was Jurgen Glick, the same Jurgen Glick who wrote about the prince for all the European magazines.

Dan snapped his fingers. "*Looking for his golden moment!* Remember? That was the phrase he used a couple of times in that article. This Glick guy knows what Rainer's after. He's known all along."

Shelby thought it all raised another question. "Are they working together or against each other?" The picture implied they were friends. The last article suggested that maybe they weren't.

They notified the police and went back to watching the game. Dan didn't pay any attention to the TV. The Golden Room was on his mind. He was trying to figure out how to get into Eckert House without anyone knowing he was there. After the mistakes he made in the Music Room and the Garden Room, he thought it was best not to raise everyone's hopes.

Dan decided to wait until Wednesday, Uncle Jeff's day off. It was also the day Miss Alma and Mrs. Doheny would be up on the third floor answering letters and paying bills.

Dan always let himself in through the back door, and that's what he did the following Wednesday. He snuck past the security guard and slipped into the library.

Dan located the architectural drawings from when the mansion was expanded in the late 1870s. He was interested in a very specific spot: where the basement under the original section of Eckert House met the basement under the south wing of the mansion.

There, three separate chimneys met. There was also a room just beneath the kitchen, once used as a pantry for vegetables and fruit.

The other thing that Dan knew—and most people did not—was about the space between the walls at the back of the "new" section. It went deep underground and had no logical connection to any other concealed passageway in the house.

It took a few minutes, but Dan confirmed what his own rough sketch had shown: the measurements did not add up. There was a large space unaccounted for.

"Now, how do I get in?" Dan wondered aloud.

When the mansion was converted from a private home to a museum, the pantry just off the kitchen was converted into a security station. Studying the original plans, Dan first thought that the entry to the Golden Room was through that space. But if that had been the case, then the entrance would have been discovered during the remodeling.

"It has to be through the other pantry just below it," Dan whispered. He had no clue how to find the secret entrance, but knowing that somehow he would, he grabbed a flashlight and set off.

The entrance to the lower pantry was at the back of the large closet in the kitchen. A wall of shelves swung out, and a steep staircase wound down into the dark. Dan closed the door behind him and crept down into the cool depths of the pantry.

The space was about twelve feet by twelve feet. Even though it was no longer used to store food, the old shelves still lined the wall.

Dan searched for some sign of a release or handle or lever that would open a concealed door. He figured it had to be on the south wall, the one made of brick. His first pass yielded nothing.

"C'mon, Pruitt, you know it's here . . ."

He tried again, this time lifting the old shelving units one by one. About halfway through, he dropped his flashlight. It blinked out. Dan reached for it in the darkness and found it. But some impulse kept him from turning it on. He decided to wait a moment instead.

What is it? he asked himself. Why are you waiting? A second later he realized why. There was a sliver of light along the floor of the south wall. The light grew brighter as a door opened. A figure was silhouetted against the golden sheen that glowed from the room behind the wall.

"I was wondering how long it would take you to find it, Mr. Pruitt," said a familiar voice. It was Miss Alma. "Come in."

LIGHT

Words could not begin to describe the beauty of the room into which Dan stepped. The flames in the kerosene lanterns that Miss Alma used to illuminate the space were caught by the shiny gold that covered every inch of the walls and ceiling and reflected back millions of times. It was dazzling. Dan's first thought was that this was indeed what heaven must look like. He couldn't speak.

"I suppose I should thank you," Miss Alma said. "When Mrs. O'Hara made that comment about the storm cellar, your face told me everything I needed to know."

Miss Alma now believed that Julius Eckert had always intended to keep this room a secret. It was something just for him. The new part of the house was designed with the idea of placing the Golden Room underground—and keeping it there. "I was starting to wonder why there were no stories about it being here," she continued. "No rumors. Nothing. I don't know how he did it, but he did."

"All of this just for one man?" Dan was amazed. "Think of all the life that happened upstairs . . . the summers and winters, the comings and goings. And all the time this incredible treasure was so close, and they never knew it."

Minutes went by without their speaking. Dan circled the room touching the molded figures all done in gold. The wall depicting fire was especially impressive. The way it reflected the light made it seem like the flames were moving.

"When did you find it?" Dan asked Miss Alma.

"A few hours after you left on Saturday."

"Now what?" Dan asked after another lengthy silence. "Do we get in touch with another museum, do we call the newspapers, do we—"

"No!" Miss Alma shouted, her eyes wild. Dan was shocked by the outburst. Rather than apologize, she continued in the same frantic tone. "Do you realize what this is? Historians have been searching for this room for decades. People were killed because of it. It's worth hundreds of millions of dollars, if not more. If we let anyone know it's here, what do you think will happen? Not just to Eckert House, but to the entire town? Do you think we could begin to have enough security to protect it? And then there's Rainer Leopold prowling around the place. What about him?"

Dan was taken aback. He had never seen Miss Alma in such a frenzy.

"So you're just going to leave it here?"

"For the time being, yes. And I hope I don't have to remind you just how important it is not to say a word about this to anyone."

Dan assured her he'd keep quiet.

"*Anyone*," she repeated.

Over the next week, Dan noticed a change in Miss Alma. She was often missing. Mrs. Doheny or Uncle Jeff would hunt for her, knowing for certain that she was in the museum, but not be able to find her. Dan knew where she was, of course, and once he snuck down to the hidden room to gently remind Miss Alma that she was needed upstairs. It seemed to Dan that she was obsessed with the Golden Room.

In a way, Dan knew how she felt. Not that it was all he thought about, but never before had he carried around a secret like this. He knew the location of something that treasure seekers, historians, princes, art lovers, scholars, and detectives had tried to find for years. It gave him a real lift and felt cool.

"What's up with you lately?" Shelby asked him. "You've been strutting around school like you own the place."

"Oh, sorry," was all Dan could answer. And he meant it. He didn't want to give anything away.

But it was difficult. He kept coming back to the word "cooler," and he realized how it would be so much better if he could share why he was feeling so cool. Not that he wanted to make himself better than anyone else . . . No, he wished all his friends could stand in the middle of the Golden Room and feel the history and see the beauty, too.

When an entire week had gone by and Miss Alma still did not offer any plans for dealing with the Golden Room, Dan felt he had to bring up the subject himself. He'd given it a lot of thought and had even done a little creative exploring.

Dan didn't want to go back into the secret spaces of the mansion, areas where he had nearly been killed. There were just too many memories he didn't want to face again. But he also realized that he had a responsibility to Eckert House and even, in an odd way, to history. He had to make sure the Golden Room was safe.

Rainer Leopold had been looking for the room for years. And now he had found it. He didn't know it yet, but he had. Dan didn't trust him. Once Leopold confirmed the Golden Room was in Eckert House, lawyers would get involved and the treasure would be turned over to the prince. At which point, he would probably sell it and it would vanish into the collection of some billionaire where the public couldn't appreciate its beauty. That wouldn't happen if the Golden Room was no longer in Eckert House when Rainer Leopold solved the mystery. No, it had to be taken to a larger museum, a place where Miss Alma and others could get a judge to keep it away from the greedy prince.

So on Saturday morning, when Miss Alma had once again vanished, Dan tried to figure out a way to make the Golden Room disappear.

The hollow wall at the back of the mansion plunged some thirty feet below the foundation. At the bottom of that space was a long tunnel that led to the war memorial in the park across the street. It was a tunnel Dan had found by chance and had used to escape from Rick Doheny. Dan suspected that the hidden room somehow opened into the space above the tunnel.

First, he had to get into that secret passageway. The fastest way to do that was to go in through a concealed panel in a room on the second floor which was used to display toys from the 1860s to the 1960s.

Dan timed the rounds of the security guards. As soon as the coast was clear, he tripped the hidden lever. The panel slid open, and Dan ducked inside. Getting to the spot inside the walls where he suspected there was access to the Golden Room was a matter of a few sharp turns, and then a drop.

Rungs that formed a ladder were nailed to the beams. They enabled Dan to make the descent to the spot below the kitchen where he felt the back wall of the secret room would have to be located.

"I was right," Dan whispered when he arrived at the spot. "At least I *think* so." There were no beams in an area about twenty feet by ten feet. It was only covered with boards. Ten by twenty were the dimensions of the east side of the Golden Room. Holding his breath, Dan gave one of the boards a gentle tug. It was loose.

"I think we can pull all of these right off," he said. "And if I'm right—" A noise from the other side of the wall made him realize that Miss Alma was most likely just a few feet away inside the Golden Room itself. Dan didn't want her to know where he was. At least not yet. Not until his plan was all worked out.

Dan climbed to a spot that was level with the kitchen. If his calculations were right, on the other side of the wall stood the large stove that had been brought over from England in the 1920s. Satisfied that he had it all figured out, Dan then made the climb back up to the second floor. He slipped out of the secret passageway without being seen and went down the main staircase to find Miss Alma.

Rainer Leopold was waiting in the front hall. He stood up. "Mr. Pruitt."

Dan stopped.

"I understand from one of the security guards that some work is being done to the walls in the Music Room."

Dan swallowed hard. "Well, if that's what you heard—"

"You heard correctly," said a crisp voice from the end of the hall. It was Miss Alma. "We took one of the mirrors off the wall and discovered that the plaster to which it was attached is starting to break apart. We are about to repair the walls and give the mirrors a careful cleaning."

All of this was true, but Dan was surprised that Miss Alma was sharing it. After all, the reason they took the mirror off in the first place was to look for the Golden Room.

"And just how does that concern you, Mr. Leopold?" she challenged.

"Ah, yes," he answered calmly. "That's the six hundred million dollar question, isn't it?"

Miss Alma smiled at him. "Yes, I expect it is."

"Since I'm an expert in antique glass—not to mention precious metals—I thought I might offer my services."

"I don't think I could afford you, Mr. Leopold. Eckert House runs on a very tight budget."

It was while Miss Alma and the prince were smiling daggers at one another that the entire plan dropped into place for Dan. Suddenly he knew how they were going to get the Golden Room safely out of Eckert House. He couldn't help it. He laughed out loud. It was so simple! Both Miss Alma and Rainer stopped and looked at him.

"Sorry," Dan offered quickly. Then, still laughing, he turned and exited to the kitchen.

COMPLICATIONS

"What on earth was that all about?" Miss Alma demanded a few minutes later.

"It's all too perfect!" Dan exclaimed. He then outlined his plan for removing the Golden Room. "We'll do what Julius Eckert did! He brought that thing in here in crates along with the mirrors from the Music Room. Since the mirrors are coming down anyway, we'll crate them together with the Golden Room and ship them both out together."

Miss Alma listened carefully to everything Dan had to say. The gold panels would come off the walls in sections. Then the boards on the back of the east wall would be removed. The hidden room would then open onto the concealed shaft.

At the same time, the large stove in the kitchen would be moved, and the wall behind it broken open. The panels would then be raised up the shaft and into the kitchen. From there they would be crated with the mirrors and taken out of Eckert House.

Dan felt strongly that they couldn't risk the chance that someone else would discover the Golden Room. They had to get it to a more secure location as soon as possible. The museum up in Pittsburgh was the best choice. From there a decision would be made as to where the Golden Room would ultimately find a home.

"And the best part is, you can invite Rainer Leopold into the Music Room as the mirrors are being taken off the wall. He can see for himself that there's nothing underneath. He'll go away thinking he was wrong and never bother us again!"

Dan explained that their best chance of making Rainer go away forever was to "prove" to him that there was no reason to think the Golden Room was ever in Eckert House.

"It's just what a magician does. He directs your attention away from where he wants you to look."

Miss Alma listened without saying a word. Dan had been around her a lot, but he couldn't tell what she thought of the idea. However, he knew that silence from Miss Alma was usually not a good thing. When he was finished, she said thank you, and left.

"Well," Dan said with a sigh, "I'm still alive. That's a good sign."

Dan realized that Miss Alma was ready to move forward when he arrived at the museum after school on Monday. Several workmen were out back constructing large wooden crates. When Dan went inside, he found even more workmen carefully removing the mirrors from the walls of the Music Room. Miss Alma was supervising them — at the top of her lungs. As soon as Dan saw what kind of mood she was in, he tried to duck out. Too late. She saw him.

"Mr. Pruitt!"

"Yes, ma'am."

"Go into the front hall and see if Mr. Leopold is there. If he is, you may bring him in."

Dan was surprised Miss Alma had waited for him to get there before letting Rainer see the Music Room. He guessed she had done it on purpose. After all, it was his plan.

Rainer Leopold was indeed waiting in the front hall. But, unlike all the other times, he was not relaxed. He was standing. He was pacing. A few of his hairs were even out of place.

"Hello," Dan said casually. "Miss Alma was wondering if you'd like to join her in—"

"Yes," he snapped.

The look on Rainer Leopold's face when he rushed into the Music Room was one of pure confusion. Miss Alma tried to engage him in conversation, and he tried to be polite and respond, but he was clearly not interested in chit chat. He was interested in what was on the walls behind the mirrors. As soon as he could break away from Miss Alma, he went over to inspect them. Miss Alma smiled ever so slightly at Dan.

"As you can see, Mr. Leopold, the plaster is cracking, and the mirrors were in danger of falling off. It was lucky we discovered it when we did."

"You never said how or why you made that discovery," Rainer said, turning to glare at Miss Alma.

"No, I didn't," she said with an icy smile. "It would have been a terrible loss if . . ."

Dan stopped listening. He watched Rainer's face as Miss Alma went on and on explaining how they were going to fix the walls and how, while that was happening, some of the cracks that had formed in the mirrors would be repaired by a craftsman in New York.

She also talked about how sturdy the crates being made had to be. All of it was true, for Miss Alma refused to lie. She just didn't feel it was necessary to tell him about how they were also going to ship the Golden Room out with the mirrors in those same crates.

Rainer made small talk about how difficult it was to repair old glass, then made an excuse, and left. Dan followed him to the front door. Rainer practically ran down the front steps and out through the gate.

Dan laughed.

"Don't gloat, Mr. Pruitt," Miss Alma said in a low voice. She had quietly followed him. "We're not out of this yet."

Jurgen Glick was arrested that night. The police called Dan's mother so that she could bring Dan down to identify him in a lineup. Jesse, Dylan, and Ted were there, too. When they saw Glick behind the two-way mirror with all the other men, they broke away from the police, burst into the lineup room, and proceeded to beat him up.

"I guess we can call that a positive identification," Sergeant Haines said, pulling the boys out of the room.

"You don't understand," Dan heard Glick shout as they took him back to his cell. "I'm trying to help! I'm the good guy! I know what he's up to!"

This troubled Dan. Glick sounded like he was telling the truth.

"What exactly is he charged with?" Dan asked. What it amounted to was stalking.

"The thing is, you can't really prove that, can you?" Dan observed.

They couldn't, but they could hold him for a few days while they investigated the complaint.

"But what if he's not guilty?" Dan asked.

"Then we'll let him go."

Dan dropped the subject. On the way home, his mother brought him back to it.

"What was that all about, Dan?"

Dan explained that he was convinced that Rainer was the dangerous one.

"So, because Rainer Leopold is up to no good, Jurgen Glick has to be innocent? Sorry, Dan, that's too simple. The man has been sneaking around town for too long. An innocent man doesn't do that."

She had a point. She also had something else for Dan. When they got home, she gave him a small box which contained her grandfather's belongings. "I found it this morning," she said.

Dan opened it at the dining room table. There were only a few things inside: a pair of shoes (Dan's mother thought they were the shoes he wore when he was married), an old baseball, a watch, a key (she didn't know to what), and a book of poetry.

The saddest of all was a picture of him in his uniform, standing in the back yard with his wife, Dan's great-grandmother. Other than his discharge papers, the only evidence that he was in the military was a cloth hat. It was just like the one Dan wore for Scouting. It was called a garrison cap, and it looked like a rectangle before it was put on. People who worked in fast-food restaurants often wore the same style, only theirs were made of paper. Dan put it on. It was a perfect fit.

"Very handsome," his mother declared. "Should I salute you or order a cheeseburger?"

When Dan took it off, he noticed a slip of paper tucked inside the headband. He carefully removed it. It was folded over several times. After so many years, the paper was very delicate. It ripped slightly at the creases as Dan unfolded it.

The picture on the piece of paper left him speechless.

"What is it, Dan?" his mother asked.

"Mom, are you absolutely certain your grandfather died in 1947 — after the war?"

"Positive. Why?"

"I mean really, really sure?"

"Yes, Dan, look, here are his discharge papers. December 21st, 1945."

Dan was quiet. "My mistake," was all he said.

Upstairs, Dan opened the diary. He laid the piece of paper from the hat next to the sketch of Woody Woodpecker. The pictures were almost identical.

Dan would have rushed into his grandfather's room and tried to get him to talk, but Grandpa Mike had left that afternoon with Will Stoller for a week in Pittsburgh!

The next afternoon, Dan, Pete, and Shelby met at Pete's house to discuss the possibilities. Certainly lots of people drew doodles of cartoon characters;

Dan and Pete went through a phase where they drew Radioactive Rabbit on everything.

"But Pete's a better artist than I am, so they didn't look alike at all. These Woody Woodpeckers look like they were drawn by the same person."

That was true.

"Maybe they were traced," Shelby offered.

That was a real possibility.

"Or," said Dan, "Grandpa Mike . . ."

The rumble of a large truck and the *whoosh* of its hydraulic brakes as it eased down the steep hill of Filkins Street drew them to the living room window.

"Is that the O'Hara's moving van?" Dan asked.

"No," Pete informed him. Pete lived just up the street from Eckert House. "It's the truck that's going to take the mirrors to New York. My dad said it'd be here around now."

"What?" yelled Dan with alarm.

He tore out of the house, jumped on his skateboard, and arrived at the museum before the truck. Miss Alma was out front waiting.

"What are you doing?" Dan asked, half-crazed. He knew the Golden Room had not been loaded into the crates that stood sealed and waiting on the front lawn. "Miss Alma?"

"Go home, Mr. Pruitt," she said as she signaled to the truck rounding the corner. "You're not needed here."

CHAOS

The truck was gone. On it were all the crates loaded with the antique mirrors. The Golden Room was still there beneath Eckert House. Miss Alma had thrown away their one chance to get it to safety. Dan was furious.

Dan barely spoke to anyone the rest of that day. The Eenies chattered endlessly about the approaching camping trip on Friday night, so much so, that Dan couldn't take it anymore. He excused himself from the table, did the pots and pans, and then closed himself in his room for the rest of the night. He pretended to be asleep when his mother came to check on him.

The next day at school Dan was preoccupied. When his history teacher asked him to name one of the achievements of the ancient Roman Empire, he answered that they were the first to harness electricity. He got a big laugh from his fellow students, and a zero for class participation.

Dan decided he'd better talk to Miss Alma before he flunked out of school. He found her in the Golden Room that afternoon. As before, whenever he entered, he had to take a few seconds to catch his breath. Miss Alma had brought down scores of candles, and the glow was reflected back in such a way that the walls themselves seemed to generate the light. Miss Alma barely noticed Dan when he entered.

"Miss Alma, we have to talk," he said.

"It's safe," she answered. "As long as we don't say anything, nothing will happen to it."

"But for how long? I found it. You found it. Pete and Shelby aren't stupid. They're bound to figure it out. And Uncle Jeff keeps wondering where you've disappeared to. How long do you think it'll be before he puts it all together?"

Miss Alma didn't answer. She stared, unblinking, as if in a trance. Dan lost his temper.

"This isn't just for us!" he shouted. "And it wasn't just for Julius Eckert either. Do you know what this is, Miss Alma? It's a test. Maybe that's what that crazy Russian monk had in mind all along. The Golden Room is something that makes you see what kind of person you really are."

"Lower your voice, Mr. Pruitt!"

Dan took a deep breath. "You don't keep beautiful things just for yourself. It's cooler when everyone can see them. Keeping this to himself didn't make Julius Eckert a better person. I don't think this room is supposed to be hidden away. You wouldn't light one of these candles and then put a tin can over it, would you? Well, that's what you're doing."

Dan was breathing very hard when he finished. Miss Alma acted as if she hadn't heard a word he'd said. Dan realized he was powerless to change her. He also knew he had one more thing to say. "Don't worry. I'll keep your secret. But I'm sorry. I can't work for you anymore."

Dan turned to go. He got all the way out to the pantry before Miss Alma called to him. It sounded like she was crying. He stopped, but he didn't go back inside. He couldn't. She finally came out to him.

"I've been an old fool. What do I do now?"

"I don't know," Dan said honestly.

"I'm sorry, Daniel."

Rainer Leopold returned the next day. A call to the craftsman who was repairing the mirrors in New York confirmed that Rainer, pretending to be a customer, had been there when they were delivered. He saw them unpacked. He knew the Golden Room was still in Eckert House.

Uncle Jeff was told everything. Miss Alma and Dan took him into the Golden Room. Then he followed Dan into the shaft behind the concealed room to examine it. Dan shared his original plan.

"It would have worked, Dan," Uncle Jeff said. Then with a wink he added, "We're going to have to keep you on the right side of the law."

One way or another, the golden panels had to come off the walls. So Dan and his uncle examined them and figured out how it could be done. It was fairly simple because, as Uncle Jeff guessed, Julius Eckert would have had as few people as possible bring it in. "I think the four of us can take it apart," he said. He meant Dan, Pete, Shelby, and himself.

"Now all we have to do is figure out when to do it, and how to get it past Rainer Leopold," Dan added.

That was no small task.

Jesse, Dylan, and Pete's cat, Chester, provided one part of the solution the next day. When Jesse and Dylan got off the bus, Chester was waiting. Maybe he wanted to continue the chase they'd started with Jurgen Glick the week before, or maybe he was just bored. Whatever the reason, he dropped on Dylan from a tree. When Jesse tried to help, Chester attacked him.

Both boys tried to climb back on the bus, but the terrified driver, worried the cat would follow them inside, closed the door and drove on. As Dan looked back, Jesse and Dylan fell into a mud puddle. They stood up completely muddy from head to toe.

An hour later, Dan was in the Golden Room with a bucket of brown paint and a large brush. As Miss Alma gasped with horror, he slapped paint on the precious metal.

"It'll wash off," Dan promised. "This thing has to be disguised, or we're sunk." Uncle Jeff helped, adding a few artistic touches of his own. When they were done, the Golden Room looked like it had been carved out of wood. The change was nothing short of amazing.

"One problem solved," said Dan with a sigh. Now all they had to do was smuggle it out of Eckert House while Rainer Leopold watched.

Rainer Leopold was more than watching. He had come up with a new strategy. He brought an official from the International Federation of Museums with him. It was an organization that made sure museums did not display stolen works of art.

The plus-sized woman, Helga Koonzel, looked like an escapee from a bad German opera. Dan thought all she was missing was a spear and a helmet with horns. Legally, Helga had the right to wander around Eckert House and ask questions.

She did. That meant the task of getting the Golden Room out was now almost impossible. The Eenies came to the rescue.

At dinner that night, they continued their non-stop rant on the only subject that interested them: the campout. They wanted to know whether or not they'd be able to use the bathrooms in Eckert House if there was an emergency.

"Why would you need the bathrooms in the museum if you're up at Camp Willowbrook?"

Because, they told him, they were camping in the park right across the street from the mansion.

"All twenty of you?" Dan asked, excitement building. The answer was yes. Plus four leaders. Dan kissed each of them and ran to call his uncle.

Pete and Shelby were brought into the plan as soon as school was out. There was no time to spare, and they'd have to work hard if they were going to pull it off. Of course Dan's friends were disappointed that they hadn't gotten to see the Golden Room in all of its glory.

"This is how it's going to work," Dan explained. He launched into the plan. During the day, Uncle Jeff had removed the painted panels from the walls and ceiling, and had taken down the flimsy wall that opened into the shaft. Now they were going to lower the panels four feet and then carry them down through the stone tunnel that led to the war memorial in the park across the street.

Throughout the afternoon and evening, Uncle Jeff, Dan, Pete, and Shelby took the panels into the tunnel. This underground passage sloped down and met a flight of steep stairs that took them even deeper. The steps ended in a long, flat bottom passage that was, thankfully, no longer full of water (as it had been only weeks before). It led to another steep staircase which climbed up to the hollow interior of the war memorial. They stacked the panels at the bottom of the second staircase.

It was hard work, made even harder because it had to be done in complete silence, for Helga Koonzel was prowling through the museum over their heads. Rainer Leopold was with her. Miss Alma's job was to keep them as far away from the back of the mansion as possible.

By nine o'clock that night all the panels were out of Eckert House and at the bottom of the staircase below the war memorial. Dan, Pete, Shelby, and Uncle Jeff took a well-earned rest. Above them they could hear a chorus of young voices singing "There Was An Old Woman Who Swallowed a Fly." Everything was going according to plan.

"What's next?" asked Pete.

Next was a hayride for the girls. Four large flatbed wagons filled with hay were on the street in front of the park. Soon teams of horses would be hitched to the wagons, and the girls would be pulled all over town singing, as Dan put it, "more dopey songs about people swallowing weird things."

While the girls were gone, they would carry the panels up the stairs, through the hidden door on the monument, out into the park, and hide them in the bushes.

"It's risky to have them out in the open like that," Dan added, "but we just don't have a choice. And hey, what's a bold plan without at least one part that gets your heart beating a little faster?"

"My heart is beating fast enough as it is, thank you," Shelby shot back.

"When they get back," Dan said, ignoring her, "and the horses are taken away, we wait until things quiet down. Then we load the panels onto the wagons. We cover them with hay and wait until tomorrow morning when the tractors come and haul them back out to Bradley Farm."

Uncle Jeff explained that a truck would be waiting there. The panels would be transferred into it and driven to a museum in Pittsburgh. Once there, lawyers would take over to protect the Golden Room. They were sure Rainer wanted it just so he could resell it.

Everything went as planned. The panels were well hidden in the bushes before the girls returned. Then, shortly after midnight, they were loaded onto the wagons and covered with hay. No one, including Dan's mother who was only fifty yards or so away, knew they were there.

Shelby, Pete, and Dan each took a wagon, covered themselves with hay, and tried to get some sleep. Uncle Jeff stayed awake to keep watch. Dan couldn't resist making a comment.

"Don't mean to make you nervous or anything, Uncle Jeff, but do you realize that we're sleeping on a six hundred million dollar mattress?"

"You know, Dan," he whispered back, "I knew I wasn't going to get any sleep tonight. You just made sure I wouldn't get any for a month."

"Just doing my part."

The wind kicked up during the night. It looked like rain. Just before sunrise, Uncle Jeff woke them, and they moved off to a spot in the bushes where they could keep an eye on the wagons without being seen. Dan was sure that he wasn't the only one nervous that a work of art worth six hundred million dollars was lying unprotected and out in the open.

As the little girls came out of their tents to make breakfast, the wind picked up even more. It started to blow the hay off the top layer of hidden panels. First one was exposed, then another, then another.

"What do we do?" Dan asked.

"Stay exactly where we are," his uncle ordered.

He pointed. Rainer Leopold and Helga Koonzel had arrived to continue their torment of Miss Alma. They waited at the gate, directly across from the wagons. A piece of hay actually blew into Rainer's hair. He plucked it away, irritated. Another piece hit him in the face. He looked annoyed and started to cross to the wagons.

Just then Miss Alma appeared. She opened the gate and let them in. As Rainer and Helga stormed up the front walk, Miss Alma cast a worried look first at the wagons and then toward the bushes where they were concealed.

"Hang in there, Miss Alma," Dan murmured. "We're almost done."

But they weren't. Uncle Jeff made a call on his cell to the man who was scheduled to come pick up the wagons. One of the tractors was broken. He wasn't coming until much later. As they learned this, it started to thunder. It would soon be raining.

"If we don't get those panels somewhere else before it starts raining, all the paint is going to wash off," Dan said with real panic in his voice.

"Even if it does, Rainer still doesn't know they're out here," said Shelby.

"And we have to keep it that way," Dan answered. He took his uncle's cell phone and made a few calls. The message was simple: meet in the park as soon as you can. Bring every ball, bat, slingshot, and potential weapon you can carry.

Just then the Scout troop started singing, and Dan realized he would need them as well. He felt like a chef who was being asked to make a gourmet dinner without being told what the ingredients were.

Then the miracle happened. The final ingredient. A moving van pulled up in front of the O'Hara's. It maneuvered into position at the curb, and the four-man crew opened the doors on all three sides. They threw the thick blankets and old quilts they would use to wrap around the furniture onto the sidewalk.

By the time they were through, Dan had shared his plan with Shelby, Pete, and his uncle. Right on cue, a small band of well-armed kids (led by Jesse, Dylan, and Ted) had arrived. It was time to begin. Once again, why Dan needed help wasn't important. Dan was who he was, and that was good enough for everybody there. *Very cool,* Dan thought. *Maybe I'm getting this God thing after all.*

It was time to begin.

Objective number one: get Uncle Jeff on the truck and acting like he's part of the crew.

Objective number two: get as many blankets off the sidewalk and over to the wagons as possible.

Objective number three: get the panels wrapped in the blankets and onto the moving van.

Objective number four: keep Rainer Leopold and Helga Koonzel as far away from the front of Eckert House as possible.

Objective number one proved to be easy. The driver and one of the crew were in the house with Mrs. O'Hara. Uncle Jeff walked onto the van and apologized to the rest of the crew for being late. He then gave them some money and told them to go up the street for coffee. He promised to get things ready while they were gone. The movers hurried away.

Objective number two was tougher. And it had to be done bit by bit. Jesse, Dylan, and Ted, along with three others, jumped on their bikes, formed a line and headed for the blankets and quilts piled on the sidewalk. It was precision riding, and they were good.

Whoosh, a hand shot out as the first rider sped by. One thin blanket snatched. *Whoosh*. An old quilt. *Whoosh*. Another quilt. All six came away victorious. They tried a second pass. Six more blankets and quilts were lifted with ease. A third pass yielded four more.

Shelby and Pete were at the wagons with two other boys. They started removing the panels and wrapping them in the blankets.

Meanwhile, Uncle Jeff motioned for two other boys, Shawn and Josh, to creep under the van. As soon as they were in position, he threw some mattress boxes onto the street. The boys picked them up and carted them over to Shelby and Pete. This was repeated several times. The mattress boxes were the perfect size for concealing the panels.

Another pass at picking up blankets was a disaster. Mrs. O'Hara emerged from the house just as Dylan, now first in line, was about to pick one up. She screamed at him just for being near her house again. Startled, he skidded to a stop, toppled off his bike, and the other five riders piled into him. It looked like a bad day on the NASCAR track.

Claire Jamison, Ted's older sister, and her friend Kerry decided to get creative. They knew there weren't enough blankets and boxes to cover the panels, so they walked over to where the girls were breaking camp, smiled, mingled, made small talk, and started picking up collapsed tents, sleeping bags, and loose quilts. Then, just as cool as could be, they carried them to Shelby and Pete.

It was time to start moving the panels onto the van. Dan organized a line. Fortunately the moving van blocked the view from the O'Hara's house. Uncle Jeff was there at the open side door. He lifted the panels up and in, strapping them to the walls of the truck.

It was when half the panels were loaded that disaster struck again. Dan kept a close eye on Eckert House, and he spotted Rainer Leopold peering out a window on the second floor. If he didn't know what was going on that split second, Dan knew that he'd figure it out—and soon.

Time for reinforcements.

Dan ran over to where the campers were eating a hasty breakfast so they could clear out before the storm started.

"Guess what?" he shouted, getting everyone's attention. "I've hidden a special prize in the big house just across the street. I'll give you a hint. There's a man inside who looks like a movie star. It may be hidden on him. On your mark, get set, go!"

It looked like the start of the Boston marathon. Twenty screaming girls dropped their food and sprinted across the park toward Eckert House.

"Daniel?" questioned his mother.

"I'll explain later, Mom," he called out as he followed the girls.

It couldn't have been timed better. Rainer Leopold was just coming out the front door as the girls reached the gate.

"That's him!" someone screamed. They swarmed. Rainer retreated. They all followed him inside.

Dan ran back to the group loading the panels. He told them to forget wrapping them, just get them on the van as quickly as possible. He figured he'd bought them ten minutes at most. After that, he wasn't sure what he'd do.

It started to rain. Hard. There were five panels still on the last wagon. As the rain pounded down, it washed away the paint. The gold was there for everyone to see.

"Would you look at that," said Jesse.

"Is it real?" asked Dylan.

"I liked it better brown," Ted offered.

"I think it's perfect the way it is," said a deeper voice. It was Rainer Leopold.

The girls poured out the front gate. Rainer was torn between running for his life or staying and claiming the object of his life's quest. He chose to stay.

It wasn't pretty. Especially after Dan told the girls that the prize was inside the ruby on Rainer's ring.

"Hurry!" Dan shouted to his friends. He couldn't count on the girls keeping Rainer tangled up forever.

"Where are we going with this?" asked a man with a deep voice who had walked around the van to join them. It was Jurgen Glick. The police had released him.

Dan froze. He didn't know what to do.

"I hope you have a backup plan," Glick continued. "Prince Charming will follow this moving van wherever it goes."

"Well . . ." Dan started.

"Let's just get it loaded onto the truck," Jurgen interrupted. "I'll take care of His Highness later. He thinks he has a moral right to this, which is funny since he's going to sell it to some billionaire in South America who wants to impress his girlfriend. No, he won't get his hands on this."

Just how they'd keep that from happening was unclear. The whole plan was based on Leopold not knowing the Golden Room was in Eckert House, let alone packed inside the O'Hara's moving van.

Jurgen helped them finish loading up the panels, all the time keeping an eye on Rainer, who was taking a pounding from the little girls.

The noise had drawn the driver and Mrs. O'Hara outside — even in the rain. The rest of the crew returned with coffee and doughnuts. The little girls attacking the strange man set Mrs. O'Hara off, and when she saw Dan, she started yelling at him again.

Now excitement of any kind was known to draw Chester to investigate. And since he lived just up the street, he was there in a moment. Dan was the first to see him. Mrs. O'Hara was second. She screamed and hid behind the driver. The driver, a nervous man, screamed and hid behind Dan.

Dan knew better than to scream. He ducked behind one of the wagons and hoped for the best. As he hid, Dan saw the driver hop inside the cab of the truck and pull away. Uncle Jeff was still inside. He gave Dan a "thumbs up" as the truck roared past.

SOLUTIONS

Prince Rainer Leopold the Fourth of Penrod-Holtz was arrested after he threw Claire Jamison and Kerry into the lake. The police didn't buy his story that he was the victim. It made all the papers, and once again the media questioned why this sleepy little town attracted so much international attention. Miss Alma certainly wasn't about to tell them.

Dan, who was once again the hero, decided that enough was enough. Being famous was a drag. He liked being just Dan. That was way cooler.

Dan's friends had a few questions about what they'd been involved in. Dan launched into a long and involved explanation that he hoped would bore them. It did. They didn't even let him finish.

Rainer Leopold's arrest had a positive outcome. He couldn't stop them from getting the Golden Room to a safe place.

The surprise of the day was the discovery that Jurgen Glick was a descendent of King Wilhelm of Norvania. He felt that his family had a stronger claim on the Golden Room than Rainer's.

Rainer and Glick had been friends in college and had even shared their hopes of someday finding the lost treasure. But then Glick realized that the prince only wanted it for selfish reasons. From then on, he'd spent his life shadowing Rainer, hoping to keep up with him, and maybe even discover the Golden Room first. Glick felt the Golden Room should be shared with the world.

Glick really was just trying to warn Dan about Rainer, even though he went about it in the wrong way.

Once Uncle Jeff stopped the moving van's driver, he convinced him to make the quick trip to Bradley Farm where some of the other security guards were waiting with a truck. The Golden Room was safely taken to Pittsburgh where it was stored in a vault. It was left to lawyers and experts to argue about who really owned it.

Helga Koonzel hadn't wasted her time after all. It turned out that a bag of marbles once owned by an Eckert child in the 1920s really belonged to Albert Einstein. She was convinced they were stolen. Miss Alma let her take them. She figured Helga had lost enough of her marbles already.

So that was that, Dan realized. It was over.

Except for the diary. Dan needed to finish that. The Golden Room Caper (as Dan, Pete, and Shelby privately called it) helped Dan make the last connection. When the police arrested Rainer (and Mrs. O'Hara—she wouldn't stop yelling), Jesse started singing his favorite movie theme song and marching around.

"C'mon, Dan," he shouted. "It's 'The March of the Robots' from *Mega Wars*. We won! Celebrate!"

That was the last piece of the puzzle for Dan. The march was exactly the beat of the piece of music the boy had written in the diary, the music they had played and beat out so often. The time signature was a "2" over a "4." Two-four time. A march. March was his grandfather's last name. The notes weren't important, but the rhythm was.

But how did the diary get into Eckert House? Dan had to wait until Sunday afternoon when Grandpa Mike and Will Stoller got back from Pittsburgh to find out. Everyone was there to welcome them home: Dan, Pete, Shelby, Uncle Jeff, and Miss Alma.

Miss Alma claimed that she wasn't there for any particular reason, but Dan noticed how she asked Pete to move so she could sit on the couch next to Will. She even squeezed Will's arm when he said how good it was to be back in Freemont. Everyone thought it best that Dan talk to his grandfather alone.

The conversation was slow and deliberate, but Dan only saw the positive in that. Four months ago Grandpa Mike couldn't talk at all.

As soon as Dan brought out the diary, Grandpa Mike began to shake. Tears gathered in his eyes.

"How?" he asked.

Dan told him. Grandpa Mike nodded as if the book ending up in Eckert House was logical. With great difficulty he opened to the last page of the journal. He read it to himself.

"Stopped here. Father's plane shot down . . . missing in action . . . probably dead."

"But he didn't die, right? He came back."

Grandpa Mike nodded. "Thought dead . . . left this in park . . . at monument . . ."

Someone from Eckert House must have found it and brought it home, Dan concluded. It was that simple.

"So angry," Grandpa Mike continued. "So bitter . . . even more two years later . . . car accident . . ."

Dan thought of the scared little boy his grandfather was so many years ago. A boy whose emotions were so much like his own.

Grandpa Mike spoke with great conviction. "Don't be bitter, Danny. Don't be scared. Not what God wants, no matter what. All of us in God's hands. Your father, too."

The room was swimming through the tears in Dan's eyes.

"I miss him so much, Grandpa. Why can't he come home?"

"Don't know," Grandpa Mike answered honestly. "Still miss mine . . ."

Grandpa Mike was crying, too. Dan put his arms around him.

"Make him proud."

"I will," Dan promised.

Smarter, stronger, deeper, cooler. Dan knew he'd never stop trying.

What is  SOUL GEAR ?

Based on Luke 2:52:
"And Jesus grew in wisdom and stature,
and in favor with God and men (NIV)."

2:52 is designed just for boys 8-12!
This verse is one of the only verses in
the Bible that provides a glimpse of Jesus
as a young boy. Who doesn't wonder what
Jesus was like as a kid?

Become smarter, stronger, deeper,
and cooler as you develop
into a young man of God
with 2:52 Soul Gear™!

Zonder**kidz**

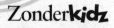

The 2:52 Soul Gear™ takes a closer look by focusing on the four major areas of development highlighted in Luke 2:52:

"Wisdom" = mental/emotional = **Smarter**

"Stature" = physical = **Stronger**

"Favor with God" = spiritual = **Deeper**

"Favor with men" = social = **Cooler**

2:52 Mysteries of Eckert House

Three friends seek to uncover the hidden mysteries of Eckert House in this four-book series filled with adventure, mystery, and intrigue.

2:52 Mysteries of Eckert House: Hidden in Plain Sight [Book 1]

Written by Chris Auer
Eerie stories surround the old Victorian mansion-turned-museum known as Eckert House. But what was once thought to be fiction may prove to be fact after twelve-year-old Dan Pruitt makes a gruesome discovery.
Softcover 0-310-70870-2

2:52 Mysteries of Eckert House: A Stranger, a Thief & a Pack of Lies [Book 2]

Written by Chris Auer
Many secrets lie within the walls of Eckert House, but no one is prepared when a stranger, claiming to be the sole heir of Eckert House, shows up.
Softcover 0-310-70871-0

2:52 Mysteries of Eckert House: The Chinese Puzzle Box [Book 3]

Written by Chris Auer
Dan and his friends discover a riddle hidden in an ancient Chinese puzzle box, but someone is trying to get them out of Eckert House. Whoever it is will stop at nothing to get rid of them!
Softcover 0-310-70872-9

Available now at your local bookstore!

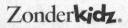

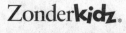